8—

My Denali

EXPLORING ALASKA'S FAVORITE NATIONAL PARK WITH HANNAH CORRAL

KIMBERLY CORRAL
WITH **HANNAH CORRAL**
PHOTOGRAPHS BY **ROY CORRAL**

ALASKA NORTHWEST BOOKS™

ANCHORAGE ◆ SEATTLE ◆ PORTLAND

*To Ben with love, may you always
feel at home in Alaska's wild lands.*

—Mom, Dad, and Hannah

My Denali was created as a labor of love with support,
guidance, and encouragement from our family of friends and
relatives, with special acknowledgment to the Carrick Family,
Kim and Melanie Heacox, and Fred and Randi Hirschmann.

Library of Congress Cataloging-in-Publication Data
Corral, Kimberly, 1962–
    My Denali : exploring Alaska's favorite National Park with Hannah Corral / text by Kimberly Corral
with Hannah Corral : photographs by Roy Corral.
        p.   cm.
    Summary: Explores Alaska's Denali National Park and Preserve and the many
kinds of wildlife found there.
    ISBN 0-88240-467-9 (hardcover)
    1. Denali National Park and Preserve (Alaska)—Juvenile literature. 2. Natural history—Alaska—Denali
National Park and Preserve—Juvenile literature. [1. Denali National Park and Preserve (Alaska).
2. Natural history—Alaska. 3. National parks and preserves.] I. Corral, Hannah. 1983–   .
II. Corral, Roy, 1946–   ill.   III. Title.
F912.M23C67 1995   95-21169
917.98'3—DC20   CIP

Originating Editor: Marlene Blessing
Managing Editor: Ellen Harkins Wheat
Editor: Carolyn Smith
Designer: Elizabeth Watson
Map: Vikki Leib and Steve Podry

Photos. *Jacket: (front)* Midnight fly casting at Wonder Lake, *(front inset)* Admiring mountain avens, *(back)*
Investigating wolf prints on McKinley River bar. *Page 1:* Airborne on a windy ridge. *Page 2:* Sun shines past Ben's
bedtime. *Page 3 (map):* Wandering caribou bull. *End papers:* Alpenglow on Mount McKinley.

Alaska Northwest Books™
An imprint of Graphic Arts Center Publishing Company
Editorial office: 2208 NW Market Street, Suite 300, Seattle, WA 98107
Catalog and order dept.: P.O. Box 10306, Portland, OR 97210
800-452-3032

Printed in Korea

NATIONAL PRESERVE

NATIONAL PARK

to Fairbanks

McKinley River

Toklat R.

East Fork

Teklanika R.

Savage R.

OUTER RANGE

Nenana R.

Healy

PRIMROSE RIDGE

WYOMING HILLS

Toklat R.

Teklanika River

Sanctuary River

Park Hdqrtrs

Visitor Access Center

Kantishna

Igloo Creek

Sanctuary R.

Jenny Cr.

Riley Creek

Wonder Lake

Wonder Lake

Toklat

POLYCHROME PASS

Polychrome Rest Area

Riley Cr.

Eielson Visitor Center

HIGHWAY PASS

Stony Hill Overlook

ALASKA RANGE

Cantwell

8

DENALI HWY

NATIONAL PARK WILDERNESS

MOUNT McKINLEY
20,320 ft.

NATIONAL PARK

3

GEORGE PARKS HIGHWAY

ALASKA RAILROAD

N

W   E

S

10 km   20

0

10 miles   20

0

Park Road closed in winter. Private vehicles
restricted beyond the Park Headquarters.

NATIONAL PRESERVE

to Anchorage

▲ Campgrounds
■ Ranger Stations
□ Visitor Centers
  & Rest Areas
● Cities

DENALI
NATIONAL
PARK AND
PRESERVE

RUSSIA

ARCTIC OCEAN

ALASKA

CANADA

Fairbanks

BERING SEA

DENALI
NATIONAL
PARK AND
PRESERVE

Anchorage

Juneau

GULF OF ALASKA

◄ MOUNT MCKINLEY'S NORTH FACE IS REFLECTED IN WONDER LAKE.

▲ WE SEE MOUNT MCKINLEY FROM OUR TENT DOOR.

A mosquito buzzes inside the tent. I try falling back to sleep, but it lands on my ear. "Buzz off!" I say, brushing it away. This time the mosquito flies toward me like an arrow on target. My only escape is to climb out of the tent. Ben, my four-year-old brother, is still asleep and scrunched at the bottom of his sleeping bag. It's morning at Wonder Lake campground in Denali

5

EVEN WHEN EATING, MOOSE ARE ALWAYS ALERT FOR DANGER. THESE TWIN CALVES FIND SAFETY NEAR THEIR MOTHER. SHE WILL CHARGE WOLVES, BEARS, OR PEOPLE THAT GET TOO CLOSE. THAT'S WHY IT'S BEST TO WATCH MOOSE FROM A DISTANCE. WHEN CALVES GROW UP, THEY'LL FIND COVER IN SPRUCE FORESTS, BRUSHY HILLSIDES, AND RIVER DRAINAGES. IF THESE TWINS SURVIVE, THEY MAY LIVE 10 TO 20 YEARS.

National Park and Preserve, and this is my last summer trip to the park before starting seventh grade.

"Wake up, Benji!" I say. "I want to show you something. Hurry up, before the sun gets any higher!"

Ben slowly crawls out of his warm sleeping bag and puts on a sweatshirt.

"There, look!" I say, pointing to the snowy peaks of the Alaska Range glowing in the rising sun. The air is cool and moist, and the sky is clear and blue. Ben is more interested in food, and strolls over to the picnic table. I follow behind him, picking ripe blueberries for my cereal.

Sounds seem sharper in the cool stillness of the morning. So when something rustles leaves nearby, I stop eating and sit very quietly. "Shhh, listen," I say to Ben.

"Hey, Hannah, moose!" he shouts, as a brown cow bolts through the brush with her long-legged calf.

The two moose stop at the edge of the campground to munch on willow leaves. Ben and I sit side by side with our breakfast watching them eat, listening for other familiar nature sounds in the ponds around Wonder Lake. *Crack! Splash!* A beaver slaps the still water nearby with its flat tail. Then, *ah-oo-oo!*

THE BEAVER IS NORTH AMERICA'S LARGEST RODENT. IT'S A GREAT SWIMMER, LIVING IN LAKES AND PONDS AROUND DENALI. WEBBED HIND FEET WORK LIKE PADDLES, AND A LARGE FLAT TAIL STEERS LIKE A RUDDER. THIS BEAVER'S HEAD IS ABOVE WATER, BUT IT CAN CLOSE ITS NOSE AND EARS WHEN IT DIVES UNDER.

7

COMMON LOONS ARE DIVING BIRDS THAT WINTER ALONG THE COAST. THEY MATE FOR LIFE AND RETURN TO THE SAME BREEDING AREA EVERY YEAR. IN DENALI, LOONS NEST ALONG LAKE OR ISLAND SHORES AND EAT SMALL FISH. SOFT DOWNY FEATHERS KEEP CHICKS WARM. THEY LEARN TO FLY JUST BEFORE WINTER ARRIVES.

Ah-oo-oo! The haunting call of a loon echoes across the misty lake. Benji looks surprised; that's a new sound for him, but a favorite for me. I can hardly wait to share more of Denali with Ben on our hike today.

Denali is a great place for kids to find adventure along rivers, valleys, and mountain tops—or just outside the tent door. I love camping in Denali any time, even when the temperature drops below freezing. You may think it's strange, but I like it when cold air leaks into my sleeping bag and tickles my bare ankles. I have a special feeling for this place, and sometimes think of this park as *my* Denali. But Denali really belongs to everyone—even kids like my little brother!

AUTUMN HIKES ARE MOSQUITO-FREE AT THOROFARE PASS!

A COLORFUL WORLD EXISTS BELOW YOUR KNEES. I FOUND THIS CUSHION OF MOSS CAMPION BLOOMING IN EARLY JUNE ON THE TUNDRA. MANY OTHER WILDFLOWERS ARE FOUND THROUGHOUT DENALI. LATE JUNE TO EARLY JULY IS THE BEST TIME TO LOOK FOR THEM, BUT SOME CONTINUE TO BLOOM LATER. A GOOD GUIDE BOOK WILL HELP YOU LEARN PLANT NAMES. ENJOY THESE FRAGILE BEAUTIES WITHOUT PICKING THEM.

I was only two weeks old the first time I visited Denali. Now I'm twelve, and I still haven't seen it all. Denali National Park is huge, with more than 6 million acres. That's even bigger than the *entire* state of New Hampshire—or Connecticut, Delaware, and Rhode Island combined!

Most people come to Denali to see wild animals and Mount McKinley, but you don't have to look far to find something to explore. Sometimes, I don't notice the tiny wildflowers sprinkled on the tundra until I sit down right on top of them. I roll onto my stomach for a close-up look, touch the soft, tiny leaves, and push my nose against the petals to smell them. Shooting stars smell like grape bubble gum. Others don't smell at all. I never pick the tundra wildflowers. I admire them where they grow, sometimes sketching flowers and leaves in my journal with colored pencils so I can identify them later.

Like the pattern in a kaleidoscope, the colors of Denali change with each turn of the seasons. Autumn begins with patches of yellow, green, orange, and red across the land. In winter, the northern lights, or *aurora borealis,* shimmer in ribbons of red and green across the night sky. When spring arrives, flocks of migrating geese and cranes honk overhead, flying in great V-shaped

◄ A DALL SHEEP EWE AND HER LAMB PREFER THE SAFETY OF DENALI'S RUGGED HIGH COUNTRY WHERE THEY CAN FLEE FROM PREDATORS.
►► BEN AND I EXPLORE WILDFLOWER MEADOWS AT HIGHWAY PASS. WHITE MOUNTAIN AVENS AND PINK WOOLLY LOUSEWORT COLOR THE TUNDRA IN EARLY SUMMER.

MOUNT MCKINLEY JOINS US FOR BREAKFAST.

14

formations to their nesting grounds. In summer, the sun shines almost all night, and the land warms quickly. Muddy rivers flow like chocolate milk, hauling away glacial silt and dirt from the hillsides. Green leaves seem to burst from their buds overnight. Baby animals enjoy the warmth too—bear cubs wrestle, Dall lambs frolic, caribou calves romp, and wolf pups chase each other. But the cold is never far away. By the end of August, summer's bloom begins to wither. Winter returns quickly to freeze the land.

After breakfast, Ben and I help wash the dishes and get ready for a long day hike. I stuff my rain gear, water bottle, and lunch into my backpack first, then my journal and sketching supplies. Benji packs his gear too—toy binoculars, sunglasses, gummi worms, and plastic cowboys. He slips on his tiny pack, and we're ready to go. Today we are planning to hike a three-mile trail to the McKinley River, a new area for me to explore. My dad says the wide gravel bar is a good place to look for wolves.

Although people rarely see wolves in the park, we always watch for them. Sometimes we see their tracks in the mud. I feel lucky if I see just one wolf in the summer. And once in a while, you might even hear them. I'll never forget one cold October night in Denali. My family and I stood beside the fire to keep warm, roasting one side of our bodies while the other side froze. The campground was empty and quiet, and a million stars twinkled in the sky. Suddenly, a deep howl broke the silence. A wolf! Soon other wolves joined him, howling in joyful harmony. They howled on and off for nearly three hours. I don't know if

A STORY UNFOLDS AS WE FOLLOW WOLF TRACKS.

16

THIS LONE WOLF WATCHES DALL SHEEP ABOVE THE TOKLAT RIVER. THE SHEEP ARE A SHORT DISTANCE AWAY BUT THE CLIMB IS TOO STEEP. THE WOLF WANDERS INSTEAD TO FOLLOW A COUPLE OF CARIBOU ALONG THE WIDE RIVER BAR. THEY ALL DISAPPEAR BEHIND A MOUNTAIN WHERE THE RIVER BENDS.

they were howling to celebrate a hunt or to gather other pack members. But I do know that if I were a wolf that night, I would have thrown my head back and howled too. We never did see the wolves, but I liked knowing they were there.

Ben and I lead the way to the trailhead. We find a bright orange sign that warns hikers to watch for a grizzly bear in the area. Grizzlies wander freely throughout Denali, eating plants and berries to fatten up for their long winter sleep. Sometimes grizzlies search for arctic ground squirrels, or hunt young moose and caribou. Once, from the safety of the park bus, I watched a grizzly chase a nervous moose away from her newborn calf. The

DENALI GRIZZLIES ARE THE SAME SPECIES, *URSUS ARCTOS*, AS THE BIGGER COASTAL BROWN BEARS. AS OMNIVORES, GRIZZLIES EAT PLANTS, AUTUMN BERRIES, ARCTIC GROUND SQUIRRELS, AND OTHER MEAT WHEN THEY CAN GET IT.
▶▶ CARIBOU BULLS ENCOUNTER DAY HIKERS ON THE PARK ROAD.

bus passengers held their breath as the bear dragged the calf across the road. I wanted to shout "No," but instead I squeezed my mother's hand to hold back the tears. I remember now what she told me then: "Denali stays wild because of life-and-death struggles between predator and prey." She explained, "One day, that grizzly's remains will nourish other wild creatures in the park." As I think about what she said, I see that Denali is special because it's one of the few places in the world where nature is in balance.

Although the bear that was seen on the trail could be long gone, we decide to keep our distance and hike somewhere else for today. I'm disappointed, but my dad explains he doesn't want the family to take any unnecessary risks. Maybe we can hike there tomorrow. I take Benji's small hand and we head in another direction.

We spend the morning hiking along the rolling tundra dotted with ponds. The sun is high when we stop for lunch. I pull bagels with cheese, oranges, and trail mix from my pack. Gummi worms dangle from Ben's lips as I hand him a bagel. I hear a *click, click, click* sound. At first I think my dad is taking pictures again, but his camera is in his pack. *Click, click, click!* I look around again and see nothing.

"Hannah, caribou!" Ben shouts. A bull walks up the hill toward us, but stops when he sees us. Startled, he stands just a

◄ SPECTACULAR VIEWS DRAW
MANY PHOTOGRAPHERS TO
DENALI AS IN THIS AUTUMN
SCENE AT POLYCHROME PASS.
► ► A BULL MOOSE SHEDS
ANTLER VELVET IN EARLY
SEPTEMBER. ONLY BULLS HAVE
ANTLERS. EACH WINTER,
AFTER THE AUTUMN RUT,
ANTLERS FALL OFF AND GROW
BACK LARGER IN SPRING.
ALASKA MOOSE ARE THE
WORLD'S LARGEST DEER.
► ► ► SNOW COVERS THE
ALASKA RANGE ON AN
AUGUST HIKE.

few yards away from me, watching us look at him. No one moves. Then, with his head high, he prances right by me, his hooves *click, click, click*ing as if to say, "Step aside, please." And I do.

Caribou are always on the move in search of food. They migrate between winter feeding grounds and summer areas where calves are born. The caribou we see here belong to the Denali herd. A ranger once told me that 50 years ago, more than 20,000 caribou roamed the park. But the herd size dropped as

20

low as 1,000 animals a few years ago. The changing size of the Denali herd is a mystery biologists are trying to solve.

The afternoon is hot. We pack up lunch and walk downhill to the ponds, following a narrow game trail littered with piles of moose droppings. We can hear the sound of water pouring and dripping. We stop to listen, but hear nothing. Then again, suddenly, water is pouring and dripping. When we reach the end of the trail, we see a bull moose with huge antlers, chewing water plants in the middle of the pond. Then he drops his heavy head to get another mouthful of food. Moose can be dangerous if you approach them, so we watch quietly for a moment before returning along the same trail. As we back away, I try to guess the size of his antlers by spreading out my arms, but my reach doesn't even come close.

MOUNT MCKINLEY, 35 MILES AWAY, DWARFS A PARK SHUTTLE BUS.

RED EYE COMBS MARK MALE WILLOW PTARMIGAN. IN SPRING, MALES GUARD OVER GROUND-NESTING FEMALES FROM SPRUCE TREETOPS, SCOLDING INTRUDERS WITH *GET-BACK, GET-BACK, GET-BACK.* WILLOW PTARMIGAN ARE ALASKA'S STATE BIRD.

Hot and tired, we leave the moose pond and walk toward the park road to catch a shuttle bus heading east. My dad flags down the bus, and the door slides open. There's room for four.

Even though we're on a bus, the wilderness is just outside our window. A passenger spots Dall sheep high above the road on a steep rocky slope. These white sheep can be mistaken for distant snow patches—until they move. Ben hands me his sticky yellow binoculars, but I'm already looking through mine.

"Those are rams," I tell Benji, "because their horns are thick and curly. The king of the hill is usually the ram with the biggest pair of horns."

Dall sheep are at home on the rugged mountains where they can escape wolves and grizzlies, but they sometimes have to cross the grassy lowlands on their way to other feeding areas. These wild sheep are always alert to danger and ready to make a quick escape to higher ground. Hungry predators aren't their only worry: many of the old, young, and weak sheep die when winter snows make food hard to find.

We get off the bus at Stony Hill Overlook, a place where there's a good view of Mount McKinley—if it's out. On clear days, buses stop to let people take pictures. The mountain looks so close, but it's really 36 miles away. Many people never get to see it because clouds hide it most of the time.

There are no clouds today, so Benji and I run to a little creek below the overlook to cool off. Before I can take off my boots and socks, Ben is standing up to his knees in the creek wearing only his T-shirt. My feet and ankles are numbed by the icy water, but the sun warms the rest of my body.

A red fox laps at the water a short stretch away. She sees us but doesn't seemed frightened. I watch as she leaps across the

RED FOXES ARE ACTIVE HUNTERS. THIS ONE CARRIES AN ARCTIC GROUND SQUIRREL. THEY ALSO EAT PTARMIGAN, EGGS, HARES, MUSKRATS, VOLES, INSECTS, PLANTS, AND EVEN ROTTING MEAT. FOXES BELONG TO THE DOG FAMILY LIKE WOLVES AND COYOTES.

WE MOVE DOWN THE TRAIL AFTER A COOL DIP.

creek and returns with an arctic ground squirrel clenched between her jaws. Then she drops it, and continues to go back and forth across the creek until she has five squirrels in a pile. The fox opens her mouth wide to scoop up all the limp squirrels. What a sight! She must have hungry kits waiting back at the den for her to return with their meal.

I quickly reach for the journal inside my pack to write this down, first recording the date, time, place, and weather. It's fun to flip through the pages and remember things exactly as I saw them. An entry from last year reads:

July 17, 1994   Polychrome Pass
3:15 p.m.   Partly Sunny

Mom and I climbed to a ridge above Polychrome Pass today. A hoary marmot stood on a rock pile watching us huff and puff our way to the top. Suddenly a golden eagle sailed right by us. There we were, eye to eye with Denali's largest bird of prey! Mom and I dropped our jaws. We looked for the marmot, but it was already hiding.

I close my journal and put on my socks and boots, ready to explore around the creek. My mom waves for us to follow her on the tundra to check out the last of the wildflowers. "It seems a

◄◄ FOR SAFETY, I STOP TO LOOK FOR GRIZZLIES BEFORE HIKING FARTHER.

◄ HOARY MARMOTS HIBERNATE IN WINTER AND LIVE ON ROCKY SLOPES IN SUMMER. THEY BLEND EASILY WITH LICHEN-COVERED ROCKS, AND BURROW QUICKLY TO AVOID PREDATORS SUCH AS GOLDEN EAGLES.

THIS BUTTERFLY, *PARNASSIUS PHOEBUS*, IS ONE OF 80 KNOWN SPECIES NATIVE TO ALASKA. LOOK FOR IT ON SUNNY WILDFLOWER MEADOWS AND OPEN TUNDRA FROM JUNE TO AUGUST ON WARM, CALM DAYS. MOVE QUIETLY AND SOFTLY TO WATCH THEM.

little late in the season for moss campion to be blooming, but look at this," she says, pointing to a milky white butterfly sunning its wings on the tiny pink wildflowers. "I don't know what kind of butterfly this is. I've never seen one like it. We'll have to look it up when we get home."

On hands and knees, we all watch the butterfly while my dad takes pictures. "Beautiful," he says over and over, looking through his camera. This discovery is a perfect way to end the day.

A bus is fast approaching, so we scramble up to the roadside to catch a ride back to Wonder Lake. It's been a long day, and I'm hungry for dinner. The ride is quiet, except for Ben, who snores as he sleeps. I look out the window to ridges and valleys I haven't yet explored. Mount McKinley towers above all the other mountains. The Native Athabascan people of this region named the giant mountain *Denali*, which means "the high one."

And it is—Denali is 20,320 feet high at its south peak, the highest mountain in North America.

Even though Denali is covered in ice and snow year-round, it looks different all the time. My favorite season is early autumn, when morning fog rolls up the McKinley River and hides Denali's north face. By noon, the sun burns through the fog to reveal a crown of shining white peaks. At sunset, if the weather holds, the mountain turns cotton-candy pink with alpenglow until the black of night covers it again. As always, from her mountain throne, Denali watches like a queen over this wild kingdom.

As our bus returns to Wonder Lake campground, puffy clouds creep over the mountains. We walk straight to the food locker and pull out macaroni and cheese for dinner. We share the cooking area with other campers. Soon everyone is swapping stories about their day's adventures.

I ask the campground host about the grizzly bear sighting on the McKinley River Bar trail. A week ago, she said, a family of hikers surprised the teenage bear eating soapberries near the river. The bear scared them with a bluff charge, but no one was hurt. The hikers knew exactly what to do. They stood their ground together, waved their arms in the air, and shouted at the bear. He took off. Since then, no one has seen the young grizzly, though people have seen tracks in the mud and old berry piles at the end of the trail.

"Let's try that trail again tomorrow," I suggest, swatting at the cloud of mosquitoes in front of my face.

After dinner, I grab my fly rod to cast for lake trout at Wonder Lake. I've never caught one, but it doesn't matter. I'd only release the fish in the lake anyway.

Back home in Eagle River, Denali National Park lies north, four hours away by car. I see Denali—*the mountain*—every clear day on my way to school. Each morning as the yellow school bus drives around the bend, I think, "There's *my* Denali." But "the high one" stands for others to see, too. I wonder what they think when they see her. When I look at the mountain, I remember all the times I've had exploring the wilderness there and know that Denali will always be with me.

PLAYFUL GRIZZLY CUBS APPEAR TO BE DANCING.